D1459517

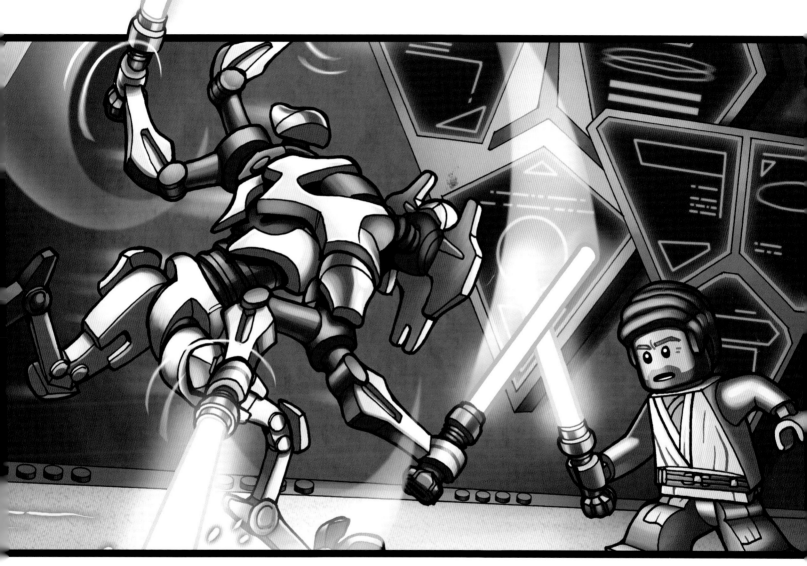

REVENGE OF THE SITH

BY ACE LANDERS   ILLUSTRATED BY DAVID WHITE

SCHOLASTIC

SCHOLASTIC CHILDREN'S BOOKS
EUSTON HOUSE,
24 EVERSHOLT STREET,
LONDON NW1 1DB, UK

A DIVISION OF SCHOLASTIC LTD
LONDON ~ NEW YORK ~ TORONTO ~ SYDNEY ~ AUCKLAND
MEXICO CITY ~ NEW DELHI ~ HONG KONG

THIS BOOK WAS FIRST PUBLISHED IN THE US IN 2015 BY SCHOLASTIC INC.
PUBLISHED IN THE UK BY SCHOLASTIC LTD, 2016

ISBN 978 1407 16263 8

BOOK DESIGN BY ERIN MCMAHON

PRINTED AND BOUND IN ITALY

2 4 6 8 10 9 7 5 3 1

PAPERS USED BY SCHOLASTIC CHILDREN'S BOOKS ARE MADE FROM WOODS GROWN IN SUSTAINABLE FORESTS.

WWW.SCHOLASTIC.CO.UK

MIX
Paper from
responsible sources
FSC® C019014

FSC
www.fsc.org

ANAKIN LOSES THE BATTLE WITH HIS FORMER FRIEND. BUMMED OUT, HE SITS TOO CLOSE TO THE LAVA AND HIS TROUSERS CATCH ON FIRE. LUCKILY, THE EMPEROR IS NEARBY AND RESCUES HIM JUST IN TIME.
I LIKE MY SITH LORDS ON THE DARK SIDE, NOT BURNED TO A CRISP!
OUCH! HOT! HOT!
SSSSS!